The Biography of a Silver Fox

THE BIOGRAPHY OF A SILVER FOX
or Domino Reynard of Goldur Town
With over 100 Drawings by
ERNEST THOMPSON SETON

University of Nebraska Press
Lincoln and London

Manufactured in the United States of America
First Bison Book printing: 1988
Most recent printing indicated by the first digit below:

1   2   3   4   5   6   7   8   9   10

Library of Congress Cataloging-in-Publication Data
Seton, Ernest Thompson, 1860–1946.
    The biography of a silver fox, or, Domino Reynard
of Goldur Town : with over 100 drawings / by Ernest
Thompson Seton.
        p.   cm.
    Reprint. Originally published: New York:
Century Co., 1909.
    Summary: Follows the activities of a silver fox as he
leaves his mother, finds a mate, establishes a den, and
outwits human and animal enemies.
    ISBN 0-8032-4200-X. ISBN 0-8032-9191-4 (pbk.)
    1. Silver fox—Fiction. 2. Foxes—Fiction. [1. Silver
fox—Fiction. 2. Foxes—Fiction.] I. Title.
PS2801.B56   1988
813′ 52—dc19   CIP 88-12143
[Fic]

Reprinted from the 1909 edition published by the
Century Company, New York.

This Story is Dedicated to the One
for whom it first was told,
Ann Seton

In this Book the designs of title-
page and general make-up were done
by Grace Gallatin Seton

NOTE

TO the reader, who would know the *motif* of this tale, I might here repeat the general preface to my first book of Wild Animal stories, but instead will give it more pointed application.

The purpose is to show the man-world how the fox-world lives—and above all to advertise and emphasize the beautiful monogamy of the better-class Fox. The psychologically important incidents in this are from life, although the story is constructive and the fragments from many different regions.

It chanced that at the time I was writing it Mr. Charles G. D. Roberts also was writing a Fox story ("Red Fox"), his a general treatment of Fox life, mine a particular phase of the same. Neither has read the other's story. Yet, I am told, one or two incidents in the Domino's life are in "Red Fox," published in 1905, and that on the other hand certain adventures which appear in my "Springfield Fox" (1898) were used in Mr. Roberts's tale. This means simply that we have independently learned of traits and adventures that were common to the Foxes of New Brunswick, New England, and farther west.—E. T. S.

List of
Full-Page Drawings

10

Part I

EARLY DAYS

I

HIS EARLY HOME

HE sun had dropped behind the Goldur Range, the mellow light beloved of the highest earthborn kinds was on the big world of hill and view, and, like the hidden lights of the banquet-hall, its glow from the western cornice of the sky diffused a soft, shadowless radiance in the lesser vales. High on a hill that sloped to the Shawban from the

The Glad
Moon

west was a little piney glade. It was bright with the many flowers of this the Song-moon time; it was lovely and restful in the neither-sun-nor-shade, but its chief interest lay in this — it was the home of a family of Foxes.

The den door was hidden in the edge of the pine thicket, but the family was out now in the open, to romp and revel in the day's best hour.

The mother was there, the central figure of the group, the stillest, and yet the most tensely alive. The little ones, in the woolly stage, were romping and playing with the abandon of fresh young life that knows no higher power than mother, and knows that power is wholly in their

15

service, that, therefore, all the world is love. Thus they romped and wrestled in spirit of unbounded glee, racing with one another, chasing flies and funny-bugs, making hazardous investigations of bumble-bees, laboring with frightful energy to catch the end of mother's tail or to rob a brother of some utterly worthless, ragged remnant of a long-past meal, playing the game for the game, not for the stake. Any excuse was good enough for the joy of working off the surplus vim.

The prize of all, the ball of the ball-game and the "tag" in the game of catch, was a dried duck-wing. It had been passed around and snatched a dozen times, but the sprightliest cub, a dark-looking

little chap, with a black band across his eyes, seized it and, defying all, raced round and round until the rest gave up pursuit, losing interest in the game they could not win; only then did he drop the wing and at once achieved a new distinction by actually catching mother's tail. He tugged at it till she freed herself and upset him by a sudden jump.

In the midst of the big, little riot, the form of another Fox gliding into view gave the mother and, by transmission, the cubs a slight start; but his familiar appearance reassured her: it was the father Fox. He carried food, so all the eager eyes and noses turned his way. He dropped his burden, a newly killed Muskrat, and mother ran to fetch

DOMINO'S EARLY HOME

it. Tradition says he never brings it to the door when the young are out, and tradition sometimes tells the truth. When mother threw the muskrat to the cubs, they fell on it like a pack of little wolves on a tiny deer, pulling, tugging, growling, rolling their eyes toward the brother they growled at, and twisting their heads most vigorously to rend out each his morsel of the prey.

Mother looked on with love and seeming admiration, but she divided her attention between the happy group about the meal and the near woods, which might contain a lurking foe; for men with guns, boys and dogs, eagles and owls, all are ready to make quarry of a baby fox. She never relaxes her vigi-

lance, and is ably backed by her mate, who, though secondary in family matters and not allowed in the den while the young are blind sucklings, is nevertheless a faithful provider of food and a tireless sentinel.

Their merry feast was at its height when the far-away *" Yur-yur-yur yap"* of the father was heard, telling plainly of approaching danger. Had the cubs been half-grown, they would have known what it meant; but being so young, mother quickly told them: translating the far barking into low sounds of menace, she sent them tumbling back into the den, where in dim light they quietly finished each the piece of Muskrat that he had secured.

AMONG the farms of New England alone there are at least a thousand pairs of Foxes. Each and every pair raises a family every year, and it is very certain that such home-scenes as this described take place by every den door at least once every fine day during the late spring and early summer. Not fewer than a hundred thousand times every year, then, it is repeated in one form or another under our very noses, and yet so furtive are they, so clever and so unremitting are father and mother, that not more than one man in every hundred thousand has the good luck to see this family group that charms us by its appeal to the eye, and touches our hearts by showing how very

near these creatures are to us in
their affections and their trials.

The lucky man in the township
of Goldur, the hundred-thousandth
man, was Abner Jukes, and he was
not a man at all, but a long-legged,
freckle-faced, straw-thatched Yankee boy, who had climbed a tree
after a crow's-nest when he should
have been bringing in the cows.

He had taken in the merry scene
below with something more than
the mere hunting instinct of a boy:
he had felt little thrills of delight
that told of a coming naturalist.
He had noted the dark cub with
the coon-like mask or domino, and
had smiled with pleasure over the
cub's exploits. He had no thought
of injuring the family or even of

disturbing their frolic, but he was the cause of its ending then, and later of a sad bereavement.

Like many of the farmer boys, Abner used to fox-hunt in the winter. He was the proud possessor of a Hound that promised to be "the finest in the State." Though only a puppy, he already was large-limbed, thin-flanked, and deep-chested. He had a voice of peculiar resonance and power, and a sullen, savage temper that boded ill in his prime. Abner had locked him up, but a chance had set the puppy free, and off he went in search of Abner. It was his near approach on his master's track that had startled the father Fox.

The mother, having seen her

HEKLA
PUPPY

seven young hopefuls safe indoors,
now ran to intercept the danger.
She deliberately laid her trail so as
to catch the Hound should he come
near the den, and in a little while
heard a brassy bellow that made
even her stout heart beat faster.

But she had no thought for herself. She led the lumbering Hound
away; then at the safe distance of
a mile dismissed him by a very simple double-back, and came again
to the den, to find all safe, indeed,
but the dark-faced cub, the one
that usually met her at the door,
was now crouching farthest back,
with his nose in the sand of the
floor.

He had been peering out when
that weird and penetrating Hound

" THE BEAST "

note came. It had sent vibrant chills down his small spine to the tip of his woolly tail; it also sent him back in haste to the farthest end of the home, where he groveled till long after the danger was over.

Men of science tell us that there is a master-chord for each and every thing, that each bell-jar is responsive to a certain pitch that, continued, can split it asunder, that the organist can seek out and sound a note that will wreck the cathedral's noblest window, that a skilful bugler can raise a strain that will shatter the nigh-looming iceberg. So also there seems to be a note that can play on the un-reasonable chords of fear, that can shake the stoutest heart; and the

dusky cub, had he been able to think of such things, must have felt that day that this was the sound to undo him,—a sound to sap the strength of his limb and heart,—this was his note of horror-thrill. His world had so far been a world of love; that day it was entered by fear.

II

TROUBLE

IT is a matter of wide belief among hunters that a Fox never harries the barn-yard next his home. He has no desire to invite vengeance from the near neighbor, so goes by preference to distant farms for forage. This may have been why the Jukes's barn-yard escaped while the Bentons' was raided again and again. Old man Benton had not large patience, and his little store was more than gone when a quarter of his fine hens had disappeared. He reckoned that he " would cl'ar the farm of shooting-irons if the boys didn't make out somehow to protect the chickens."

Si and Bud Benton were walking on the hilltop the next Sunday when they heard the voice of the Jukes's Hound on the trail of a Fox. Boys and Hound were not on speaking terms, so they did not interfere. They watched the valley below, saw something of the chase, and were delighted to note the ease with which the Hound was disposed of when the Fox was tired of the run; it would make a

capital story to tell the post-office crowd in presence of some of the Jukes.

But even while they watched, the Fox reappeared, carrying a snow-white hen and made across the valley. Benton's prize Dorkings were the pride of his heart; there could be no doubt that this was one of them, and that the Fox was taking it home. The whiteness of the victim helped the boys to keep sight of the Fox through the brushwood to the very hollow of the den, and half an hour later they were standing beside the doorway, amid snow-white thoroughbred plumes. A big pole was used to probe the hole. The curve of the burrow prevented it touching the

cubs, though they were terribly frightened, and their parents ranged the near woods, vainly seeking some way of helping them. Their earliest thought was of mother omnipotent; but this was the beginning of disillusionment: here were creatures of whom even wonderful mother was afraid.

Though it was on the Jukes's farm, the Benton boys decided to come next day and dig out the Foxes. But the mother instincts were aroused. The home had become a place of 'danger. At once she set about preparing a new den, and at dawn began to move her family.

Among the country folk, when it is decided to save only one of a

litter of kittens, there is a simple, natural way of selecting the best. The litter is left in the open field. The mother soon finds her young, and begins carrying them back to the barn; and it is believed that the first that she brings is always the best. There is at least one good reason for this: the liveliest will get on top of the pile and force itself first on mother's notice, and so be first brought back. Thus it was now. The mother Fox was met in the tunnel by the liveliest cub, the eldest and strongest, him of the domino face, and she carried him first to the safety of the new home. At the next visit his most vigorous sister, and at the third a sturdy little brother, were taken away.

Meanwhile the father was wholly occupied with sentinel duty in the neighboring hills, and day was beaming when he gave the warning just as mother ran off with number three.

The Benton boys had come armed with shovel and pick to dig out the family, and ordinarily would have succeeded in an hour; but three feet from the entrance their progress was barred by a great ledge of rock. They were debating what to do, when the sound of a blast from the quarry in the hills suggested a plan. One of the boys went for a charge of dynamite. This, with fuse and cap, was fixed in a cranny of the rock. In a minute there was a fearful shock and

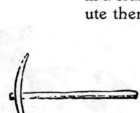

blast, the hillside trembled in a cloud of dust, and then it was seen that the upheaval had not opened the den, but had buried the tunnel in broken rocks, and that the cubs within were doubtless crushed and stifled. The shock had made a tomb of the home, and the boys went away.

THAT night, had they been there, they might have seen father and mother Fox clawing out the earth and vainly mouthing the broken granite in their efforts to reach the home den. The next night they came again. On the third night the mother came alone, and then gave up the hopeless task.

III

THE NEW HOME

THE new home of the Foxes was a mile away, and not on a hilltop, but down by the river, the broad Shawban, where it quits the hills and for a time spreads out in peaceful pasture-lands. Here in a great hollow facing the stream on a slope that was bordered by rocks all interbound with aspen roots and birch was the new-made den. Two gran-

ite slabs of rock were wardens of
the gate, for the Foxes still believed
that in the rocks lay their safety.
That earlier den was a hillside in
the pine-woods, this in a little aspen vale; the pine-tree soughs and
sighs; the aspen twitters or shivers
and rattles aloud, while the river
goes singing and tinkling. Ever
after that day of fear, the pine-song
was an evil memory, even as now
the aspen and the river sang together a song of peace.

Sloping away from the den door
was a long, smooth sward. Passing
by banks of bramble and bracken,
it dropped to a sedgy bay, where
the river paused to smile and purl.
This green slope was the training-
ground of the three, and here was

played, not once, but fifty times, that summer that old scene of the home-coming hunter laden with food. The ground was beaten with the battling of cubs and the stamping of tiny feet in mimic fight. But the little Foxes were growing fast now, the eldest fastest of all, and as he grew, his coat and the mark across his face turned daily darker.

The parents were now training them for the hunt. They were almost weaned; their food was that of grown-up Foxes, and they had in a way to find it for themselves. Father and mother would bring the new kill, and leave it not at the door, but in the woods, fifty yards away, a hundred yards away, and

more, as the young grew stronger, and then encouraged by mother's *churring* "All-well" call, they rushed forth for a very serious game of "seek or go hungry." How they raced about in the bramble cover, how they skimmed and circled on the grassy banks and peered with eyes and noses into every hole! How they tumbled gleefully over one another when the breeze brought all at once a little hint or whisper, "Come this way," and how well they learned at length to follow the foot-tracks of father and mother at full speed till it brought them to the hidden food!

This was the beginning of the life-game for them, and in this way

they were taught the real hunting.
The old ones provided abundantly,
and it seemed as though all had
an equal chance; but there are no
equal chances in life: 'to him that
hath shall be given.' The oldest
cub was the brightest, strongest,
and ablest, so he was the one that
could best find the hidden food
and therefore was best nourished;
his always were the choicest and
largest morsels. He grew faster
than the others; the difference in
their size and strength was daily
more apparent, and in yet one more
way they grew apart. His baby
coat, a dull, dark gray, grew darker.
When brother and sister began to
show the red and yellow of their
kin, he showed daily a deeper

tinge, which already on face and legs was black.

It was late July now. The old ones had not only labored tirelessly to feed the young on the fat of the farms, but had also been vigilant to ward off all danger. More than once the ringing note of the dark Hound sounded near their dale, and never failed to give the creeps to the dusky cub; but each time one of the old Foxes had gone to meet the foe, and had served him with some simple trick that sent him home defeated. They found this so easy among the river rocks that they grew over-confident; they despised their clumsy enemy, till one day while the cubs—the dark one, the slim sister, and

the little brother—were rollicking about the glade in search of father's latest kill, the brindled Hound burst in upon them. His sudden roar struck terror in their hearts. They scattered, but the little brother was not quick enough; the great jaws snapped and crunched his ribs, and the mongrel Hound carried him away, pausing once or twice to break the slender bones or grind in his bloody jaws the tender, woolly fur, but still bearing the body, till in the farm-yard he dropped it at his master's feet, and looked expectant for the praise that did not come.

Troubles never come singly. The father Fox was trotting home at dawn next day with a new-killed

duck when a clamor of Dogs sent
him round by a way that he had
never explored. It led to a high-
fenced lane that he could not scale
without loosing the duck, so he
kept on; but the Dogs were behind
him now. He rushed, alas! into
a barn-yard, into the home of another Dog, and there he died the
death.

But his family knew only that
he never came home, and their
mourning, however real, had none
of the poignancy of that which
comes to those who have seen the
loved one's tragic end. Thus the
mother and her two cubs were left
in the den by the aspen bank, and
the widow took up the burden
without fear. Her task was, in

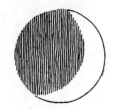

The
Red
Moon.

truth, nearly done. With August the young began to follow her on long hunts and to find their own food. By September the sister was as big as the mother, and the dark brother was much taller, as well as stronger, and clad in a coat of black. A strange feeling now sprang up between the sister and brother, and then between mother and son. They began to shrink from the big, splendid brother and at length to avoid him. The mother and daughter still lived as before,—for a time at least,— but some subtle instinct was at work to break the family bond. The tall, black Fox and they were friends when they met, yet all three seemed to avoid a

meeting. So now that he was swift and able to care for himself, Domino left the old aspen dale, with its gentle memories and the river-song, and drifted away in the life of a Fox that is alone.

IV

THE NEW GARB AND THE NEW LIFE

HIS was his entering of the larger, stormier world that lay beyond the aspen shade. Now he began life for himself; now he must rely only on his own powers for food and safety. So paying the price, he garnered the recompense, and daily developed in speed, in brains, and in beauty.

The Leaf-falling Moon.

Not long after he had quit the home den he had a brunt of chase that put his swiftness to the hardest test, that showed him legs may be slower than wits, and that brought to his knowledge a friend for the hour of peril—a friend he had seen every day of his life and had never known till now.

Pursued by a couple of Dogs, he ran round and round the rocky hills till his feet were cut and bleeding. It was a dry, sultry day, and by a great effort he got far enough ahead of the enemy to make for the river, where he might bathe his hot, weary, and bleeding feet. In the shallow margin he waded along and found the cooling waters sweet, keeping on up-stream. In this

way he had come a quarter mile when the nearing voices of the foe were followed by their appearance in plain view on the trail. Instinctively the cub sought shelter on a brushy island, and from this safe retreat he saw those Dogs run to the edge and lose the scent, work up and down, but find it not, then homeward turn at last, entirely baffled.

It did not perhaps come clearly to the Fox that the water spoiled the trail, but he gathered the idea that the river was a good place to go to when over-pressed. It proved so more than once and in different ways. On the other side, far down, was a stretch of sand that seemed to hold no trail, so told no tales.

The
Hunting
Moon

When winter came, with glare ice on the stream, he found he could run with ease on the thin sheet, which broke, to plunge a Dog in the flood. But chief help he found on a long, straight cliff, the wall of the gorge where the river leaves the hills. Here was a pathway, broad at first, then narrowing to a scanty foothold for himself,—too small for any Hound,—after which it continued to round a point, then gently climb the cliff, and reach a forest that, by any other road, was two miles from the pathway entering in.

Finally he learned that when the hunting was elsewhere bad he could always find a meal along the river. It might be a stranded fish,

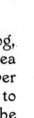

a long-dead bird, or only a frog, but still good food, and the idea within him grew, "Along the river is a pleasant place — a place to seek in every kind of strait." The river was his friend.

These were the inner changes of the Fox; these were the things that made for his success in life. And need he had of every help, for outer changes were upon him that, like the ancient noble's coat of gems, made him the magnet center of all greedy robber eyes, that set a tenfold value on his life.

The chilly autumn nights called out on him a deeper, richer robe of fur, and other powers, less comprehended, added gloss and color, intensified each day, darker and

glossier, till every tinge of red and gray was gone. And those who observe such things might have asked, "Is not this a foreshadowing of beauty yet to come? Maybe this diverse cub is predestined a Silver Fox!"

Only those wise in the woodlore of the North can fully know the magic in the name. The Silver Fox is not of different kind, but a glorified freak of the red race. His parents may have been the commonest of Red Foxes, yet nature in extravagant mood may have showered all her gifts on this favored one of the offspring, and not only clad him in a marvelous coat, but gifted him with speed and wind and brains above his kind, to guard his perilous wealth. And need he has of all such power, for this exquisite robe is so mellow rich, so wonderful in style—with its glossy black and delicate frosting—that it is the most desirable, the most precious of all furs, worth many times its weight in gold, the noblest peltry known to man. It is the proper robe of kings, the appanage of great imperial thrones to-day, as was the Tyrian purple in the days of Rome. This is indeed the hunter's highest prize, but so guarded by the cunning brain and the wind and limb of the beast himself, that it is through rare good luck more than hunter skill that a few of these fur-jewels are taken each year in the woods.

"BEAUTY"

There are degrees of rank among these patricians. They range in quality even as diamonds range, and the hunters have a jargon of their own to express all shades between the cross and the finest silver black.

His quality may scarcely· show in summer, and a Silver cub, while in the nursery coat, might pass for a common Fox. It is the approach of winter that brings out the beauties of the gifted one; and when that autumn wore away on Goldur Town with frostier nights, the Domino's darkening winter coat grew every day in richness and in length, the great tail fluffed out white-tipped, the black mark across the eyes turned blacker, like a mask,

Long Night Moon

with an emphasis of silver hair enframing it about. The head and neck grew glossy black; then, like bright stars besprinkled on the night, came shining tips of white on the inky depths, and those who had seen only the dusky cub of July would never have recognized him in November, for the noble was wearing his splendor now, the Domino stood in his winter robe, a magnificent Silver Fox.

V

BEAUTY AND THE BEAST

T soon became known that Goldur was the home of a Silver Fox. This genius of his tribe, this wonder in fur, had been seen more than once, and it was believed that many times Jukes's Hound, dark Hekla, had pushed him hard on the runway. At least the Jukes said so, though the neighbors scoffed at the idea, and maintained that the Silver Fox

was simply making a fool of the
brindle Hound, and having humiliated him by a bootless run, could
dismiss him at will by some one of
his many tricks.

A notable voice had Hekla. It
was full, deep, and so resonant that
on still nights it could be heard for
miles, and so spontaneous that he
could not help bellowing at every
jump, even when he ran his own
track back to find the way home.
The Jukes boys thought him a marvelous Hound, a paragon; but the
neighbors said he was a cross between a fox-trap and a fog-horn,
with the biggest part fog-horn, and
a sullen, savage brute into the bar-
gain. The impartial agreed that
he was a large, swift, savage half-

bred Hound with a peculiar voice,
an unmistakable voice, that, once
heard, was never forgotten. I heard
it first when he was shut up in the
barn, but it was so vibrant, so weird,
and metallic in quality, that it rang
in my ears for days afterward.

And when in the autumn, while
strolling at sundown along the
woods at the foot of the Goldur
Hills, I was startled by the same
brassy note afar, I knew it at once,
and could tell by its regularity that
Hekla was on some track. I sat
still to listen, and soon learned
more. A light rustling of the leaves
was heard, and an instant later
there loped into view a remarkable creature, no less than a coal-
black Fox. He was cantering along

easily, but stopped on a log to look back for the foe. He was fifty yards from me, but I knew the way of the Fox. I put the back of my hand to my mouth, and by sucking made a loud squeaking. The Fox turned at once and came gliding quickly toward me. He moved catlike to within twenty yards, and there stood in a pose of the most exquisite grace, head a-cock, tail curled up, foot raised, as he sought to locate the promising noise of Rat or Rabbit so near. Oh, what a robe he wore! Though yet so early, the glossy black of his fur was set off by the pure-white tail-tip and throat-spot and the blaze of his gleaming, yellow eyes, while the silver tipping of the hairs made

a shining halo about his head and neck. I thought I had never seen a more exquisite creature, and it dawned on me, not quickly, that this was the Goldur Silver Fox. I was perfectly still,—as still as he, —and, as often happens, he did not seem to realize that this thing before him was a man; but he knew very well by the nearing "brass note" that Hekla was on his track, and turned to run lightly away. As soon as he faced about, I squeaked again, and again had the joy of seeing the marvelous pose of an alert and graceful creature; but I betrayed myself by a movement, and in a flash the Silver Fox was gone.

Ten minutes later another animal came on the scene. With

measured bellowing every few feet, crashing through the brush, breaking what would not yield, lumbering and heavy, slobber-jowled, red-eyed, regarding nothing but the track on the ground, sullenly following its every turn, came Hekla, the notorious Mastiff-hound that hunted alone and when he liked, and now was trying the odds with the swiftest in Goldur Hills.

There was something uncanny about the way in which that great, hulking brute *"sniff-sniffed"* the ground and followed unerringly every turn in the Fox's track. There was something eery in the thought that he could tell which way that Fox went. And yet he did, nor ever ran the back track.

I squeaked to the Hound, but I might as well have squeaked to a barnacle. His only thought was that trail, till it should lead him to the one that made it; and what then, I might judge by his evil red eyes and the bristling mane along his spine. I had been a fox-hunter myself, and had learned to love a foxhound; but the sight of the splendid creature that day pursued by a very hellhound, remorseless, tireless, inevadable, gave me a feeling as of seeing some beautiful bird of song being crushed by a poisonous reptile. The traditional league of man and Dog was then and there forgot. Thenceforth my heart was all with the Silver Fox.

VI

DOMINO'S WINTER LIFE

WINTER came on, and with it the irregular, unsportlike fox-hunts that the farm-boys get up — hunts in which three or four Dogs are followed not by mounted men, but by lads with guns. Once a real hunt with a pack of Hounds picked up his trail; but Domino took refuge in the rocks along the river, and profited by

every run, in that he grew stronger, as well as wiser, in the secrets of the trail. He was learning another lesson, the mastery of himself. The big Hound's voice had lost nothing of its black-art potency, but he was schooling himself to resist, and courage grew with his strength.

He lived the ordinary life of a lone Fox now, not inhabiting a den, —Foxes do not use the den much in winter,—but sleeping out in exposed places, where his thick fur robe and ample muffler-tail were protection from the cold, and his senses could guard him from prowling dangers.

His sleeping was done almost entirely by day and in the sunlight:

this, indeed, is an unwritten law of Foxes. "The night is for hunting, the sunlight for sleep." When the shadows followed the sundown, Domino would go forth in his daily quest for food, just as all his forebears had done, prompted as they were by the inborn thought called instinct, and the outborn from his cubhood's training.

It is a mistake to suppose that any wild animal can see in black darkness. They need light; much less, of course, than mankind do, but they must have some. They can *grope* in blackness better than a man can; still, it is groping. They do not love the noon-glare: their time is the soft half-light of morning and evening. In moonlight or

when starlight and snow are there, they find that all night long is a soft and pleasing twilight. So when the sun was gone and the right light came, the Domino Fox would set out on his daily quest for food.

Now he would go trotting in a general up-wind course, turning aside to examine every promising thicket and sedgy hollow, going to all the places where in the past he had had good luck, and calling at prominent posts, boulders, and fence-corners to see if any other Fox had been there of late; for Foxes, like Dogs and Wolves, have a way of making record at all the recognized signal-points of the range. Then he would go trotting

along the ridges that enabled him
to watch both sides, trying the
breeze for promise of food, stop-
ping at the slightest click of leaf
or twig, standing motionless a minute till he had satisfied himself
that it was nothing of moment, or
else creeping up cat-like to the cause
for a better scrutiny. Sometimes
he would climb some sloping tree
or perch on a high stone wall to
command a better view, or, failing
these, would make an observation
hop like a spring-bok. On these
night excursions he was far from
avoiding the dog-protected barn-
yards. It is a remarkable fact that
Foxes increase with settlement
of the wilds, because every farm-
house is really a source of sup-

plies, and has one or two regular pensioners in the tribe of Reynard.

So Domino's course was from one farm-house to another, in spite of the inevitable Dog. There were two methods of approach. One, when there was open a safe retreat, in which case he went with the utmost silence; and the other, in which he feared the Dog. Here he stood off at a distance and barked a defiance. If the Dog came rushing out, he made off; if there was no reply, he knew the Dog was somewhere indoors. Then he would sneak up and ransack such buildings as were open. Of course the best possible prize was a fat chicken, silenced as soon as caught by a dexterous neck-nip.

Long-Night Moon

But he knew enough to be content with anything that came, from a scrap of bread thrown out to the hens, to a dead rat flung from the granary rat-trap. He was not above picking out morsels from the pig-trough, and more than once, when hard pinched, he played prodigal son, and filled his belly with the husks that the swine did eat.

Nearly, but not every, night he found forage; nevertheless, five good meals a week is all any one needs to keep fat, and winter wore along.

VII

DOMINO FINDS A MATE

NO wild animal roams at random over the country. All have a home-region, a hunting-ground that they consider theirs. For this they will fight, and on this they resent the coming of any kindred stranger. Many observations show that the range of a Fox in rough country is a radius of three or four miles from a central point. It is quite prob-

Snow Moon

able that he is not exclusive owner.
Other fox-ranges may overlap this;
but he soon gets acquainted with
these established neighbors; he
learns their looks and their foot-
scents, and they pass one another
unnoticed. It is quite different
when a stranger appears on the
range. Then is invoked the primal law,

> Might is right,
> Move on or fight.

As the Snow-moon waned, the
Domino Fox in glorious fur and
pride of strength began to realize
that he was very lonely. At times
this new hankering for company
would prompt him to sit on a bank
near some barn-yard and listen to

the Dogs, if not too dangerous, or to tempt them to run after him. Or else he would tarry on a hilltop by moonlight and utter the long, barking wail that is called by bookmen the bark of the Dog-fox and by hunters the lonesome cry,

Yap, yap, yap, yap, yurrrrr-yeow,
Yap, yap, yap, yap, yurrrrr-yeow—

He poured it forth one night in the Hunger-moon, and though it was only an instinctive outburst that it was easier to yield to than to resist, he listened for the response that he did not expect, and felt his loneliness the more because he had given it voice.

The Moon now was mankind's February; the winter had broken

a little, the southeast wind was blowing softly, dankly, and in it was the
mystery called 'vernal influence'
to shape the unformed motive in his
heart, add just the shade of warmth
that turns mere smolders into flame.

Yap, yap, yap, yap, yurrrrr-yeow,
Yap, yap, yap, yap, yurrrrr-yeow —

He sang it again, and glancing
about with the ever-alertness of an
Ishmaelite free of the snow, he saw
a shadow cross a distant field of
white and vanish. He studied it
with ears a-cock and eyes aslant;
another shadow, yet nearer, went
swiftly over the snow, and Domino
sprang away in pursuit.

A man knows all his neighbors
by their looks, and is easily puz-

zled by a slight change. The Fox has a far better way. He knows his neighbors by their foot-scent, their body-scent, *and* their looks. All cannot change enough to puzzle him. In a few heart-beats he found the trail of the second shadow, and his unerring nose said that "this is the foot-scent of Blazor fox, that lives on the Shawban." Blazor had ancient hunting rights here, so Domino went on. He found the other trail, that of the first shadow, and his fighting blood was roused in a moment. It was the trail of a stranger Fox, an invader on the range, and he rapidly gave chase. But as he coursed along and nosed the trail, the anger died in his heart. Another sense he

had; more lonesome than ever he was; more eager than ever he ran; for that inscrutable, wonderful guide, his nose, was whispering: "Make haste! This is what you yearn for; this is the trail of—a lady Fox."

He bounded eagerly along, but came once more on the track of the neighbor Fox. He, too, was pursuing that trail. What a new feeling now came over Domino! Back a little he had passed the neighbor's trail with utter indifference; now what a change! It filled him to overflowing with malignant hate, no less, and his mane stood up from his ears to the little crest on the base of his tail.

Three or four fields were passed

when Domino came on the two.
It was neither a race nor a fight,
nor was it clearly peace or war
between them. The new-comer,
a small red lady with an elegant
ruffle of white, would run a little
way; Blazor would pursue and
quickly overtake, when she would
turn and snap at him. He would
bound back, but make no counter-
snap. Thus they went zigzag-
ging, and Domino, coming up, felt
a fiercer storm of mingled anger
and desire. He somehow felt he
had a claim on Snowyruff's notice,
and was not a little dashed to find
her shun him even more than she
did his rival. Domino turned on
him with a savage growl; Blazor threw up his tail, braced him-

self, and, snarling, showed a fierce array of teeth.

For a moment they stood facing each other. The little lady took advantage of the moment to make away. The rivals followed fast, menacing each other as they ran; but Domino was first to head the fugitive. She stopped and snarled, *not very hard.* Blazor was on the other side. Both Snowyruff and Domino threatened him. The rivals closed in fight. Blazor went down, and lay there snapping his teeth. Domino stood over him, but did him no great harm. The snow lady ran off. The two pursued again. They were running now, one on each side of her, growling across at each other.

But whenever did the female heart resist both prowess and beauty combined? As they cantered across the field, she swung away from Blazor and *a little nearer* the Silver Fox. All three pulled up and faced, not now as three, but a *pair* and a *one,* and the tall, black Fox of the pair stood very high upon his legs. He fluffed out his ruff and raised his great tail. Thus towering, he growled deeply, showed the gleaming rows of perfect teeth, walked stiffly toward Blazor, while Snowy-ruff came close behind, and Blazor knew it was finished. He turned and sullenly glided away.

This was the mating of Domino; this was the wedding. In no essential feature did it differ from the

weddings of men; and the mysterious guide which brought these two lives together erred not: each had what was lacking in the other. In this union they were as one compounded of twofold strength and gifts, as we shall see in the desperate days ahead.

Part II
TWOFOLD STRENGTH

82

VIII

SPRING

SPRINGTIME beamed on Goldur heights with browning hillsides, with unbound rivers, with clack of Flickers, or loud tattoo, and whistle of Hyla-peepers in every icy pond.

In the winter woods the winter-green peeped forth like cherries of the snow, and holding up their shining leaves, they seemed to say, "This is what we were waiting for;

for this our berries were red."
The Partridge and the Squirrel and
the early Woodchuck reveled in this
Crow-moon feast, and lovers of the
wilds found a pleasant thought in
this, that the All-mother had fillẹd
the seeming gap with things so
good for food. There were be-
ginnings of wooings and longings
in wood and on lake that told of
life and lives and coming life; and
in the hearts of Snowyruff and
Domino these found a deep response.

For ages the beasts have been
groping for an ideal form of mar-
riage. All the schemes of human
reverts they have tried, and all
found wanting but one. The only
plan that has satisfied the highest

requirements is pure monogamy.
This is the wed-law of all the highest kinds. The love-time fever
passes, but another bond remains.
The love-fire of the Foxes had paled
a little with the waning of the Hunger-moon, but a more abiding sense
had supervened, even as the sunset
red on the hills may seem more
generous fire than the soft red of
the granite; but one is there a
splendid moment, the other forever
and evermore. Love and friendship men call them; and though
the flickering red light blazed so
bright at times, it was the pale rock
red that gave its color to their lives.
Domino and Snowyruff were not
only mates, but were friends for
life; for such is the way of the

noblest beasts, such is the way of Foxes.

When first the snow banks gave birth to little chilly rills, the pair had gone searching, trotting, and searching ; or more truly perhaps, Snowyruff had searched, and Domino had followed meekly. Through the sandy tract east of Goldur Hills they went. There they found the little signals of other Foxes, saying in plainest Fox, " Strangers coming here must fight." Now they passed through all the upper hills of Goldur, where the snow was far too deep, and back to the riverside, and at last came to an aspen-dale, the same old aspen-dale of Domino's youth, and here the little lady

"SNOWYRUFF"

seemed to end her quest; here surely was what she sought.

She nosed this way and that, then in a thicket of hazel she began to dig a hole. Deep snow and deep leaves there covered the ground or she could not have sunk the shaft. But instinct, or some other inexplicable guide, had set her digging at the one possible place; elsewhere all was hard with frost. High on a near hill sat Domino, sentinel and guard. After an hour's digging she came out and Domino took her place. So they worked from time to time.

In a few days the den was completed—a long tunnel that ran down, then up to a chamber, with another tunnel that led, after some

yards, to a side pocket forming a smaller chamber, then turned upward till again it reached the frozen ground, where it stopped for the present.

But each day the She-fox scratched at the frozen crust overhead. Each day it melted more, till at last she forced the tunnel through, and made a neat, round doorway under a sheltering tussock of last year's grass. Now she closed the original entrance. There was no earth about the new hole; no eye could detect it, though within a dozen feet, and the growing grass made it daily better hid.

Food was no longer scarce, and once, when not hungry, having se-

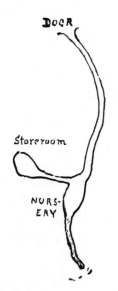

DOOR

Storeroom

NURS-
ERY

cured an imprudent Woodchuck that went a-gadding by night, she buried his fat body in the dry sand of the side chamber.

The pair were more and more careful now not to be seen near the den. Many times Snowyruff waded a hundred yards up a little rill so that there might be no tell-tale foot-scent leading home. More than once Domino lay flat on a log or crouched in the grass, while a farm-boy tramped past within twenty yards, never suspecting that a Fox was near; of such the Silver Fox felt daily a deeper distrust.

One day a different meeting came about. A human being was seen approaching. It was not a Hunter; it was one of the Un-

hunters, a young one, one with a long robe that showed feet, but no legs. On its arm it carried a basket. Domino felt not alarmed, but uneasy. He did not know that this was only a school-girl picking wintergreens; yet he felt less fear as she came nearer. He stood still; then knowledge came, a message from that untaught, unacquirable insight of the speechless ones which said, "This is a harmless human; this is a friendly one." Drawn by a feeling new and strange, he walked openly, quietly, toward the girl. She stood and gazed with fearless wonder, and with a little warm feeling growing in her heart. She wanted to stroke that glossy fur; he wanted her to stroke it.

So these two drew together. But, alas! the new friendship was broken up before established. The child's small Dog, left behind, came running now with unbounded energy and limitless indiscretion, rushed forward, barking like mad, and Domino loped lightly, contemptuously away. The girl went home with her berries and told a strange tale of a shining Fox whose eyes were only kind—a tale that none but the very young and the very old believed; that is, those who understood the child, and those who understood the Fox.

IX

THE EVENT

KUNK cabbage and hellebore were forgotten as events. Liverleaf and adder's-tongue were winning a hearing for the tidings that they bring, and as the Grass-moon followed the Crow-moon, an influence filled the air, the woods, the ground, with fecund promise of wild life renewed. And then came a change in Snowyruff. She avoided Domino as

though he were an enemy. When he tried to follow into the den, she savagely warned him to keep away. This was puzzling; but the tall black Fox was of a race that had learned to respect the she one's way simply because it was the way of the she one, and this, though on the lowest and most animal plane, is surely the foundation-stone of chivalry. He kept away from the den for days, and during that absence the great event took place.

Who is it bids the human mother love and fondle and feed the new-born babe? Who guides her hand to lift it gently, wisely? Who teaches her to keep it warm, to shield it from all danger with her body, or to buy its safety with her very life? Who is her teacher? Not another woman; not any human mind. The untaught savage mother does the same as the wisest of our kind. And call this teacher any name you will, it was the very same that taught that little mother Fox. Alone, alone by preference, was she in that dark den when the hour appointed came. All that the most skilful, wisest could have done, was done by herself, that in all her previous life had had no knowledge of this time.

Five little Foxes there were, small, shapeless, "ugly," men have said, but to the mother Fox the most wonderful, precious things that ever were known, and love, new-born,

"DOMINO WAS THERE ON THE BANK, WATCHING"

heartful, overflowing, and complete
was there for them, to hedge them
about, to cherish them, and wholly
to change her life.

It was many hours before she
left them alone, and then only to
seek for herself a cooling draught
at the near-by rill. Domino was
there on the bank, watching. She
laid back her ears a little, but made
no sound and otherwise ignored
him. He crouched, with head flat
on the leaves, and she returned to
the den. That day she had no desire to eat. Next day she was
hungry, but was little minded to
hunt. Why hunt, indeed? This
very need, this very strait, had hap-
pened to every mother Fox since
ever mother Foxes were, and deep

The
vigorous
Kit

in their brain was an instinct rooted
—the habit to prepare. For this,
unwittingly perhaps, she had laid
the Woodchuck by. In this she
found her food.

Two days later, when again
forced to face the food problem,
she went to the door and found not
far away a little pile of new-killed
Mice. Maybe they were brought
there for the young. Who knows?
Of this we are sure—that they
reached and nourished the young,
though the mother it was that de-
voured them. Thenceforth every
day there was food left at the door,
or hidden in the grass or under the
leaves near by.

For nine days the cubs remained
blind, then their eyes opened; they

whimpered less; the mother went forth more confidently. Now Domino found her less disposed to drive him off; in a few more days he had joined the family group.

This was the beginning of a new experience for him. He had been quite ready to love the cubs, and coming near them warmed his heart. There are all degrees of fatherly feeling in Foxes, from that of the reprobate who forgets, to that of the faithful father who is as good as another mother, and Domino, nobler-natured than most Foxes, responded as nobly. Maybe never before had Fox cubs been so guarded or been the objects of such devotion as these that were born that spring on the Shawban, the offspring of

Snowyruff, the brood of the Silver Fox.

When they were about a month old, the little podgy toddlers first essayed to come forth into the sunlight. Their movements were slow, and they were like little woolly pigs. They were neither quick nor beautiful, but they had something else — the charm of the helpless baby; and no one could have seen the family group without realizing that charm at work. It inspired the old ones with a vague desire to lie down beside the woolly wee ones and fondle and cuddle them, as do parents of another kind; but it also held them ready to face, for the young, what they never would have dared face for themselves.

The doorway scene of Domino's early days was now repeated often. The cubs grew daily stronger and more fox-like, and the tenderness of the old ones was at its height.

Days of joy were those on the Shawban. There were the little joys of tranquil skies and gentle breezes, the bigger joys of life and strength, the stormy joy of the hunter when game is plentiful enough, and yet calls for such skill in hunting that he rejoices in daily triumph, and last the joy of something to love. These were the joys of Domino and his mate.

But we never know how high we are lifted until at least we have the chance to look over the edge and see how low we may drop. It seems a law that over the gladness of the feast the shadow of the skeleton must pass from time to time; happy the guests whom it merely passes by.

X

AN ANCIENT FOE

DOMINO was returning home one day with food. Five little black noses, ten little beady eyes set in woolly heads, were bunched in the den-door and pointed at him or at the food he brought, when there sounded near the penetrating bay of a Hound, and Domino, startled, leaped on a stump to hear. There was no mistaking that uncanny

note, the voice of his ancient
enemy. On no account must that
enemy come nearer the home-
place, and, downing the fear in his
breast, the dark Fox loped to meet
the Hound, while the mother
warned the young ones.

It was like many another chase,
but harder, for Hekla now had
reached his strength, and away
they sped. For a moment the
Hound halted at Snowyruff's trail,
but Domino showed himself and
barked defiance that lured the big
Hound on. Both were prime, and
the run was hard for an hour.
Then Domino had had enough,
and sought to shake off the Hound
as before, but found it not so easy.
Hekla had been learning, and now

DOM-INO

106

was a gifted trailer. The first and second ruses failed. Then Domino remembered the narrow ledge along the cliff where the Shawban leaves the hills, and thither led his implacable foe.

Chance or plan, who can say? The chase drew near the cliff. The Silver Fox in his glossy black was bounding on the shore, and it seemed his speed was failing. Hekla was closing, was straining, lunging and breathing hard, and still was closing. They reached the broad pathway; it seemed a trap. Then Domino went slower; the dark Hound saw the victim in sight; four bounds were all between, and the pathway narrowed. The Hound got closer still—so

close that now he knew that he had won. Another bound, the lagging Fox was almost in his reach, and again; up that span-wide ledge the hunted lightly sped, and Hekla, broad-breasted, over-broad, crashing blindly on, was smashed back by the rugged cliff, was hurled, battered and bleeding, and down— down into the icy flood below, while the black Fox watched him plunge.

The Shawban is fierce in that gorge even in summer. In spring it is a coiling, churning sluiceway. A Hound in all his strength might well have been appalled by such a plunge, and Hekla, desperately hurt, was fighting for his life. Two miles down was he swept by that

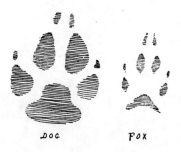

DOG   FOX

fierce flood, and it sang a merry song as it rolled and tossed about him. For two hard miles it dragged him over jagged rocks and under water-whirls, then gave a scornful swish that left him stranded on its bank, a crippled, humiliated wretch. Not that night did he reach home. Not that spring or summer did he again go trailing. Five little black noses, ten little beady eyes in innocent, woolly heads, still came to the den-door, daily, unafraid, for father was all-powerful and the den in the aspen-dale was a den in a dale of peace.

XI

THE DEER

SUMMER was at its height now, and the Rose-moon in its glory. The little Foxes had grown amazingly. Two of them were in lead-black coats that showed their noble blood, and already gave promise of future power. Snowyruff and Domino were now exerting themselves to bring home living game that the cubs might hunt and kill it for themselves.

Every day brought forth some new adventure, some curious chance, some measure of their wind and speed. Every hunt was a teacher and a trial of their hunter-craft, and nearly every day there arose some hazard in which a Fox might easily lose his life, but which left the Domino stronger, wiser, swifter than before. The upper hills of Goldur are good for Woodchucks, and Domino, one day prowling for them there among the bracken, came suddenly to a curious smell, then to a large animal crouching in the grass. It was bright reddish and covered thickly with white spots. "In the desert no one meets a friend," and Domino, instinctively freezing to a statue, gazed on

this strange creature, ready to bound aside if it should charge. The red-and-white one lay as still as death, head low, with great, round, lustrous eyes of fear gazing at him.

Deer were very rare, almost unknown, on the Shawban, so Domino had no former knowledge that could guide him. Only this became clear, the crouching Fawn was more afraid of him than he of it, and as the tense alertness of fear died down, curiosity was the uppermost feeling in Domino's brain. He moved a step toward the Fawn; it neither breathed nor winked: he took another step, was within an easy jump, but it lay as dead; yet one pace more, passing

"'IN THE DESERT NO ONE MEETS A FRIEND'"

a grass clump, he stood in full view, and the Fawn leaped to its long legs and bleating out a plaintive *meh-meh-meh-h-h-h,* it sprang clumsily over the bracken. Domino leaped high over the same place and still followed in a spirit of amusement and curiosity while the Fawn kept bleating *meh-meh-meh-h-h-h.*

Suddenly the sound of trampling was heard not far away, and in a moment the mother Deer came bounding. Her coat was bristling on her back. Her eyes were shining with a wicked, green light, and Domino realized at once that this was the form in which recurrent danger came to-day. He leaped away, but the Doe was after him,

uttering little savage, unnecessary snorts, pounding her sharp hoofs into the sod. She was nearly ten times his size, and her speed was like the wind. She overtook Domino, and made a vicious lunge with her front foot. He barely escaped by dodging. She plunged again, and again a nimble side bound saved him. This way and that the malevolent creature chased him, not content to see her young one safe and quite unharmed, but determined to kill the Fox she believed had tried to hurt her Fawn.

Then under and around the brambles and bracken she dodged and plunged, and, so far from getting tired, she seemed to gain in

117

power and wax in fury. The brambles hindering the Fox were trifles to her heavier weight; but for this, Domino might have enjoyed the mad pursuit. They had leaped about for half an hour without any change, and it was clear that while Domino might win in a hundred of the attacks, one failure might mean death. One blow of that hoof was enough to leave him at her mercy; the part of wisdom, therefore, was to reach a safer place at once. So working to the edge of the brambles, he made a dash into the open. The sprint of his life it had to be, for she was close behind him, and he barely reached the thick woods and dodged as the forefoot blow descended.

The
Unpleasant Female

But a stolid tree was the only sufferer, and in among the trunks he could scoff at the unpleasant female, and mocked at her silly, blaring Fawn. It was a lesson to be remembered — a stranger is always a foe.

XII

THE ENCHANTRESS

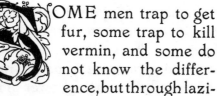OME men trap to get fur, some trap to kill vermin, and some do not know the difference, but through laziness or ignorance keep their traps out all the year around. This was the way of the Benton boys. They knew little of real trapping and always made the mistake of tying the bait on the tread of the trap. This, with other blunders, made a trap-

setting that no Fox with an atom of fox-sense could fail to detect and treat with appropriate contempt. Around the Benton traps there were no doubt three sure sources of warning for the Foxes—the smell of iron, the smell of human hands, the smell of human tracks. The last would have soon been dissipated but for the continual renewals they received from the boys themselves. The iron-smell remained, and was rather increased with each shower of rain. Domino had found all the buried traps along the range; he could go to them at any time of the day or night with much more precision than could any of the Benton boys. He visited them when they chanced to lie near his path, and from a safe

distance he looked and did things that expressed as plainly as human words could have done the scorn and ridicule he felt for such preposterously stupid efforts by such a lot of fools. Why, even the dull Woodchucks and chuckle-pated Rabbits had sense enough to scoff at Benton traps. Yes, he scorned them, but there was one thing he never failed to do when passing near—that was to turn aside to *look at them,* then leave on some stone or stump a record of his call.

It was about this time that Bud Benton got a new hint in trapping. An old woodsman from the North gave him a weird and nauseating compound of beaver-castor, anise-

seed, rhodium, worm-oil, and other potencies, reinforced no doubt with cryptic phrase and midnight ceremony. A few drops of this charm were said to be enough to draw all near Foxes and to drown all caution in them, and lead them pell-mell into any kind of a snare.

So, armed with the vial, young Benton went the rounds and sprinkled all his traps. A smell may be a faint, far sound, a still, small voice, to a human, and a very orchestral thunder to a Fox, for the Fox has a nose. But the fact of its being disgusting to a man does not in the least imply that to a Fox it would not be rose-attar, frankincense, and veritable zephyrs of Araby. The stray drops on young

Benton's clothes raised an odor that set the horses sniffing outside, and inside made his father suggest his moving to the other end of the table, at which distance it became bearably weak. But to Domino's exquisite sense that smell, borne on the wind, was as plain as a great cloud of smoke drifting along from the huge fire that produced it, and as readily followed to its source as a bugler's call or the voice of a cataract. It was world-enveloping, but it gave him no thrill of disgust. Its potency was a pleasing one, and it drew him on, as a light will draw a traveler lost in the dark, or as fairy music might lure some dreamer of the woods, and Domino, setting forth on his evening

hunt, threw up his nose to ana-
lyze the wind, then followed at a
run.

After a mile it led to a place
that he knew of old; reeking of
human tracks and hand-taint it had
been, rank of iron smell, at one
time, with a faintly apologetic little
smell from a foolish chicken head
tied to the trap.   Its place in his
mind was the memory of contempt;
but now all this was changed. As
the sunset glow can make a mud
bank blaze with splendor or turn
the clouds of pallid steam into
glorious mountains of purple and
gold, so the new and growing
power of that glamour-working
aura, that far spell, entered by his
nostrils to his soul, and there put

caution from her seat in the pilot-
house, then seized the guiding
wheel; and Domino, swinging his
ebon nose, came slowly up the
wind. It was acting like ether now,
lulling his senses and tingling in
his veins. Oh, what an exquisite
thrilling! There were suggestions
of rest after a hard run, of warmth
on a cold day, of sex-time, of fresh,
hot blood in a hungry maw, and of
many things of which he had no
previous knowledge; it was like
the opium-eater's earliest trance,
or the draft that makes the ab-
sinthe-drinker turn from the exalted
trail of those who conquer self.
Domino, with vibrant nostrils, with
beating heart, with raucous breath,
with half-closed eyes, stalked

slowly near the wonderful smell-
enchantress. He was now above
the hidden trap. He knew it, or
he knew it once, but he was in-
fatuated with the sensuous thrill,
wholly enthralled, and curious
movements of the body evidenced
the vanishing of self-control. He
longed, he yearned, he hankered
to be nearer, to enter in, to
have it enter in, to possess his
being; he wished to wallow in
it, and with strange, erotic squirms
he turned his head aside, and lay-
ing that beautiful neck on the pol-
luted soil, dragged his precious
robe in filth, rolled on his back,
and groveled in the carrion-tainted
dust. To him it was all an exquisite dream; but in the midst of

it—*Snap!* and ruthless jaws of iron had seized his back, were clutched in that rare robe of silver black, and Domino was awakened. The trance was over. Now were fully re-aroused the instincts of the hunted beast. He sprang to his feet, and as he straightened out his supple spine, the jaws of iron lost their hold, for overmuch they had seized, and Domino was free. Had it been a foothold, his doom had been sealed; but now he bounded safely away, and, blowing clear his nostrils, passed to windward and went on his evening hunt.

There are weak-minded Foxes that will come back to the evil sorceress, that will play with this death that must win; but Domino had

learned the terror hidden in that lure.

Thenceforth the smell charm conjured up amidst its many magics the deadly clutch of steely jaws.

XIII

HONEY FROM THE THISTLE

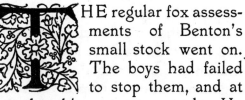HE regular fox assessments of Benton's small stock went on. The boys had failed to stop them, and at last the old man was roused. He made sundry contemptuous remarks about "when I was a boy," etc., and still further revived the memories of his youth by taking up the trapper's rôle. Traps must not be set around the farm-yard. They

work ruin among the hens; they bring disaster on dogs, cats, and pigs. The trapper must ply his craft only in the far woods. That is what the boys had been trying to do; but now the old man took up the task and went the rounds himself. At once he made some radical changes in the trap-sets — changes that might well have made the Domino shun the farm had he known and understood. First, the old man lifted every trap and smoked it with burning cedar, so that the iron smell was killed. Then he banished the smell-charm. "Sometimes it works well," he said; "but you catch the fools at once, and the smart ones soon find it out; then it only serves to warn them. There

is just one sure smell-charm for all Foxes at all times: that 's fresh chicken blood." He moved the traps from the tainted, well-known places and buried them in the dust; five feet away on every side he threw some bits of chicken, then with a cedar branch he dusted out the traces, and the snare was laid.

A few nights later Domino passed that way. For two hundred yards he had been led by the scent of those chicken baits, and as he neared the spot, his old-time caution held him to the slowest crawl. With dilated nostrils and senses all alert he came up the wind. The smell of chicken was clear. There was no odor of iron, or of man-tracks, but there was a

pungent smell of smoke, and man is the only smoky animal. There were the inviting bits of chicken, maybe dropped by another hunter; by going aside he could smell them and get away from the smoke. He hesitated, but the wind changed; all the smoky smell was gone; there was only a rich and tempting chicken breath diffusing its fragrance on the wind. Domino took three steps nearer. Now, Guardian of the Wild Things, tremble for your charge. He swung his nose in keen analysis. There was no man-scent; here was only food that he needed, good food, such as many a happy night he had eaten, and brought to the home-den. But the warning smoke-

smell, that bitter-reek, was faintly there again, and Domino took warning and slowly turned aside. Then backing out, setting down each shapely foot with care, not on broken ground, or near any bit of meat, but only on the smooth, safe earth between he went, when *Clank!* and Domino was a prisoner, not now by the broad back, where the trap was powerless, but by the foot. Yes, he was surely caught.

In vain he leaped and strained, in vain he ground his teeth on that hateful thing. The jaws of steel were fastened on his foot, were driven into his flesh, and all his efforts only wearied him and sank the iron deeper. An hour and an-

other went past in hopeless, ever-weakening struggles. All day he lay in agony, panting, at full length; then, as a mite of strength came back, rousing into impotent rage, mouthing the cold, inflexible iron, tearing with his teeth the saplings that were within his reach; turning again to struggle and strain; hoping some living thing would come; fearing some living thing might come; hoping to die; fearing to die; and hoping again. For now the dark of the end was coming over his blazing eyes. Oh, Keeper of the Wild Things, help! Why this torture, why this endless death? Surely the birthright of the beasts is this, a sudden death. So passed the long, slow night, indeed.

With the early dawn a foot was heard, was the cause of fear and hope. It might be a man, it might be his mate. She could do something, perhaps; she could at least be with him, and the tortured, draggled, and defeated Fox, low-crouching, raised his once glossy head to see not a man, not his mate, but a lurking menace, a dreaded foe—the Doe with the spotted Fawn. He lay as still as death, hoping to escape her eye; but her eyes and nose alike were keen. She wheeled with a snort; her mane, her coat, her rump, were bristling, and the evil green was like northern lights in her eye. She rushed; he dodged to the end of the chain, and here was held.

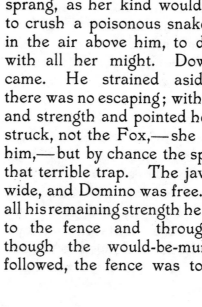

She seemed to know it; her enemy was in her power at last; her only thought was to crush him. Full of the poor courage which grows with easy victory in sight, she sprang, as her kind would spring to crush a poisonous snake, high in the air above him, to descend with all her might. Down she came. He strained aside, but there was no escaping; with weight and strength and pointed hoof she struck, not the Fox,—she missed him,—but by chance the spring of that terrible trap. The jaws flew wide, and Domino was free. With all his remaining strength he rushed to the fence and through, and though the would-be-murderess followed, the fence was too high

there to be leaped. He was weak and worn, but found it easy to slip through each time she ran around to a low place; the Fawn made a shrill cry that called the old one back, and Domino went limping slowly home.

It takes many rebukes to teach· a fool; it takes only one to add wisdom to the wise, and these two sharp lessons were enough for Domino. Thenceforth, as long·as he lived, he not only shunned all iron and man-smells, but knowing that a stranger is a foe, he feared strange odors as a new disguise of death.

XIV

SUMMER LIFE AND THE HUMAN THING

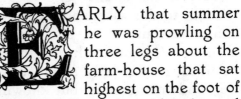

EARLY that summer he was prowling on three legs about the farm-house that sat highest on the foot of the hills. It was an old-fashioned house with an old-fashioned orchard and garden that stretched up nearly to the woods, and had cover all about. It was easy to approach the place unseen, and Domino,

DOMINO

139

prowling this way and that, sniffing his way to knowledge of all things that claimed a thought, was led through a hen-hole in the fence, into the long garden, at first among potato-vines and then in a thicket of currant-bushes and berry-canes. As he cautiously pushed through these, he sighted in the maze a black and shining *something*, very small. Still as death he stood at gaze, then slowly made it out—the eye of a Turkey sitting on her nest.

Right at the base of the tail, between brush and back, is a little bristly, emotional hair-patch on every Fox, usually of a peculiar color, but black on the Silver Fox. This was the only thing in Domino to show a change when he recognized the food prize. It bristled and stood up; but while he halted unsure, he heard another sound, and turned his head to recognize the human thing with the basket. "Oh, Foxy," she said reprovingly, "I'm afraid you are in mischief."

He did not understand, but he felt no sense of danger. He turned and, facing her, stood still, with head on one side. She walked quietly up, making low, soft sounds. He went a little back and aside. She wanted to touch him, but now the nearness of the house made him afraid. She took from the basket a scrap of something and threw it to the Fox. He nosed it, knew it for good food, took it in his teeth, and glided softly away.

That night the girl said, "Daddy, if you had a Turkey hatching in the woods, how would you keep Foxes away from the nest without hurting them?"

"I 'd put some scraps of iron around it, and no Fox would go near."

So the garden girl got a piece of chain, a broken plowshare, and a horseshoe, and set these, the emblems of friendship, labor, and luck, about the nest. Within a few days Domino came back to get the Turkey. Yes, he did. He had not the least idea of doing anything unfriendly to the human thing,— all was in the way of ordinary business,—but just before the Turkey took alarm at his approach, both nose and eyes cried warnings of

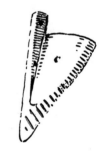

those iron-smelling things. He backed off, approached on the other side. There was another of those malevolent shiners, and caution whispered, "Go back." So back he went, and the girl would have been no wiser; but next day the father said, "Daughter, I saw fresh fox-tracks this morning among the 'tater' vines."

So Domino was tricked into letting the Turkey alone, but he found another prize—a hen on her nest, and secured her, and silenced her with a chop. He was carrying her off when he realized the impropriety of not profiting by the clutch of eggs. So he carried the hen to the woods, buried her in the leaves, came back, and got the eggs, one

by one, hid them in another place, which he marked with the musk from his musk-gland, so *he* could find it later, and another Fox would know that this was private property. Then he dug up the hen and carried it home.

Those eggs had plenty of time to run the gamut of many and mighty changes before he had need of them; but when wanted, they were there, and then he wanted them so much that their condition was a matter of indifference.

This was not the only cache he made, for although some Foxes do not hide food, perhaps because they are poor hunters and never have a surplus, a really high-class Fox soon adopts the habit, and it

grows on him. One day a month later in the autumn his eye was captured by the luscious clusters of rose-hips, unusually abundant that year. He chewed and swallowed one or two, but was not specially attracted, no doubt because he was fat and full at the time. Still, he found it amusing to jump up and snap off the red clusters. At first he merely dropped them, then he dropped them in a pile; but the instinct to hoard was stimulated and he buried the pile under the leaves, and left the musk-mark on a near-by stump. In time of need he could find that store of fruit, yes, down through drifts of snow.

XV

DOMINO'S HEIR

LAMED as he was that summer, the Domino would have made a poor run, but luckily his enemy, the swift Hound, also was a cripple. Domino had only to hunt for his brood, and the All-mother was kind; it was a year of good hunting, and daily he brought home living game. It might be only a Frog which gave the youngsters a succession of

tumbling sprints before it was caught, or perhaps a fat Field-mouse that scrambled under the leaves, and the cubs pounced on many a mouthful of sand and grass before the lucky one captured the prize. But once he brought them another kind of trainer, and the effect on the cubs was quite different.

While prowling by the river in the mist Domino saw him coming out. First in the shallow water, and then on a log, where he sat dexterously opening and eating some clams, was a huge Muskrat. His strong, yellow teeth were crunching the hinges of the clam-shells with much effect and noise. He heard nothing of the stealthy

DOMINO AND THE MUSKRAT

hunter, till there was a skurry of black fur and Domino had him by the neck. In vain he squirmed and squealed and gnashed those chisel teeth; he traveled now as he had never done before, and in twenty minutes was at the Fox's den.

The old familiar *chur-chur-chur* brought in the rollicking young ones tumbling over one another, and Domino dropped the prey. They sprang on it at once, but it was a living Muskrat, and a Muskrat is a desperate fighter. This way and that he laid about, scattering the cubs, and they danced about him like Hounds about a Bear; first this, then that, went yelping off as it felt those chisel teeth, but one there was that did not fly, not even when three

times the Muskrat had clinched on him. He was no bigger than the Muskrat, no bigger than his brothers, but he had a strain of grit. He closed again, and the others stood around. It became a duel to a finish. Instinctively he sought the vital spot; by shifting his hold as the chances came, he got nearer, and at last had his adversary by the throat. To that he held till the victory was complete, and then the family had their feast.

Father and mother had looked on. What was the feeling that kept them from interfering? Why did they not kill the Muskrat for their brood? Maybe we shall have light on this thing if we ask why a human father sets his son a task

DOMINO'S
HEIR

easy for himself, but hard for the boy.

That cub was not the largest of the lot, but he was one of the darkest. He grew up to be like his father, and those who will may read his history in the annals of the upper Shawban.

The Thunder-moon passed slowly by, and the little ones grew up. Some of them were as tall as Snowyruff now, and then began that inevitable dissolution of the family bond. First the big brother, then the sisters, lived more by themselves, did not come home for days, were more and more strangers, till the waning of the Red-moon of harvest-tide found them scattered, one and all. Only Domino

and Snowyruff were left about the
den. Sometimes together, sometimes not, for days, but always coming back, always ready to help each
other; for theirs is a law that needs
no script: these twain are one flesh.
The young ones may forget, and
must forget; the old ones are
parted by death alone.

By early autumn Domino's foot
was healed, and once again he was
the swift Fox of Goldur Hills. Once
more he was ready for the trail;
ready for the hunter, if need be.
Yes, he was even eager for the
chase. He had come to his full
power now, and his greatest gift
was his speed. There was no Fox
on the hills that could run with
him; there was no Dog that he

greatly feared. His wind seemed endless, his limbs were as sound as his wind, and he rejoiced above all things in his fleetness. It is only the swift ones that love the race, as it is the skilful *voyageur* that loves the dangerous rapids. What wonder, then, that Domino should learn to love the chase.

Thus did the Guardian of his Crystal Cup onlead him in the quest of strength and speed, forewise of that dire approaching day when strength against strength, speed against speed, life against life, he and his mortal foe should be swung in the balance together.

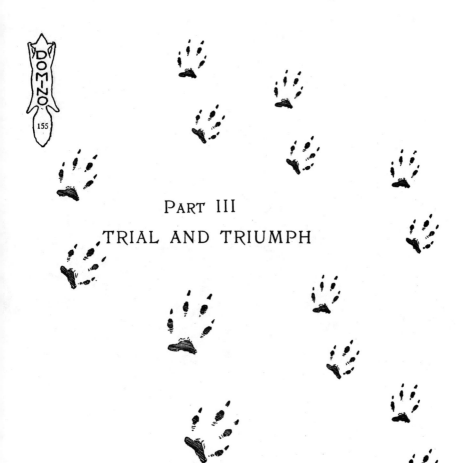

DOMINO
155

PART III
TRIAL AND TRIUMPH

XVI

THE WILD GEESE

ACH year the spring, and again the fall, brought to the Goldur Hills a few flocks of the long-necked trumpeters, that fly in the sky— the Honker-geese. They did not stay long, but there were always gunners out when a goose-flock came. Domino knew instinctively that they were good game, but one day he got better evidence: he

The Grass Moon

found a Goose newly killed. It had
escaped the gunner to die in the
swamp, so he and Snowyruff
feasted.

These Geese fed as much on
the fields as in the marsh, and
more than once the Domino tried to
stalk them, but their watchfulness
and alertness are measureless. As
well might he have tried to stalk
them while they sailed the broad
lake. Yet there is a kind of open
stalking that will bring one within
reach of the sitting bird and the
crouching hare, and which led
Domino through a stage of mental
development to a new scheme, an
improvement on the drive and am-
bush so well known in pursuing
the white rabbit. And when the

autumn came this year with the usual train of Honkers, it brought also a train of unusual experiences. A small company of the long-necks were foraging on a stubble-field by the Shawban. Domino and Snowy-ruff were together that day. They sneaked along the river-bank, through the bushes, all around the field, but found that on every side the game was guarded by open, level spaces, and at all times at least one tall neck was aloft, a conning-tower for the squad.

Then these two Foxes played a game that has been played unnumbered times, yet no man knows how arranged.

On a point of brush that extended into the field the Domino

hid unseen, while Snowyruff went to the other side and, walking into view, began a set of curious antics, rolling on the ground, throwing somersaults, lying down flat, with only her tail wriggling. The Geese turned all beaks that way, wondering what in the world the strange performance might mean.

Still Snowyruff went on tumbling and wriggling. The Geese saw nothing to fear, the Fox being so far away. Their curiosity was aroused; they stood to gaze, and Snowyruff, at the next tumble, rolled a little nearer. This she did again and again, till the old gander, always suspicious, realized that this was a ruse of approach. He said nothing, he gave no alarm, as

there was yet nothing alarming, but he moved a few steps farther away. The other Geese — his family, really — moved with him, and still that silly Fox kept rolling in the stubble like a wind-blown bundle of dry grass, or some animated tumble-weed. Yes, it was very amusing, but old Long-neck did not propose to he hoodwinked. He moved again and again, and at each insidious approach of the tumbling Fox he went still farther off. The game kept on for many minutes; the Geese had been worked across the field nearly to the edge of the stubble and were beginning to think of flight, but drew a few steps nearer to the brush, when out leaped Domino,

swifter than a hawk, and before
the Geese could spring and make
away, he had old Long-neck by the
throat.

So the hunter's crowning joy
was theirs, the long, hard quest,
the match of wits, the noble prey,
the joy of combat when you win,
the feast, the sweet content of
primal instincts gratified.

This was the best hunt together
that they had made; it helped to
bring them closer; more and more
they fought the battle side by side.
Fox unions are on a high plane,
but theirs was on the highest of
their kind.

XVII

A WEIRD CEREMONY

THE Mad-moon of the woods comes after the Falling-leaf moon. The time of erratic movement, of meaningless depressions, of hankerings that have no aim, and of passing madness. Few are the creatures that escape the weird impulses of the Mad (the November) moon. Domino was restless as it waxed. He would sit on the top of some

The Mad Moon

hill, lift his muzzle high, and utter a little sharp *"Yap-yap-yap-yurr-yurr!"* Next Snowyruff felt the same indefinable promptings; but at such times they avoided each other. At the full quarter of the moon, as Domino yapped, he heard a far-off answer. He sneaked away from Snowyruff and, trotting on, was led to the highest, baldest hill of the Goldur Range. There was an open space brightly lighted by the moon, but he stayed a while in the shade to watch. Then he was aware of other shapes at the edge of the cover. A Fox sneaked past him twenty jumps away; it was Snowyruff. Others came cautiously forward. They sat down facing one another for a time in si-

THE WEIRD CEREMONY

lence, then Domino uttered a low *churring* in his throat, raised his tail, and marched around. Another did the same; then several joined in, and ran about *churring* till the ebullition of feeling was worked off. More than once they did this, but Domino and Snowyruff passed each other like strangers. As the moon went down, the feeling died, and all scattered to their homes. It was little they did, but they had met together, and their master-thought was neither love, food, nor war. They found in some sort a joy in *being together.* We have record of such things much further pushed among beings that are higher.

XVIII

THE SHEEP-MURDERER

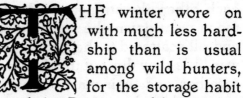

THE winter wore on with much less hard-ship than is usual among wild hunters, for the storage habit saved the Domino and his partner from famine straits, though long-cached fruit or fish is not the choic-est food.   The love-time passed, the spring was near, when one day, coming homeward over the hills, the Domino was witness of a shock-

ing crime. He was becoming a very wise Fox, and no wise Fox ever crosses a ridge without first peeping over. He slowly raised his head above the line to reconnoiter, and saw in a fenced-in, sheltered glade a flock of Sheep racing about like mad, and after them was a huge dark Hound, the one that he hated most. Two or three of the Sheep were lying weltering and dead, and as the Domino watched the brute laid another low. The plan was to seize one by the throat, throw it, and tear as long as the hot blood gushed, then seize another and another. Not horror, but curiosity and amazement, fixed the Domino to the spot. Hekla was in the midst of another fierce attack when a rifle-

shot was heard, and the ball struck
a flat rock above the murderer's
head. Who says that a Dog has no
conscience? Who dares tell that
he does not know when caught in
crime? The bloody coward knew
well what it meant; he leaped down
a sheltered gully and fled for his
life, unseen, and his master never
heard him charged with crime.
The Domino also ran away across
the field, but he was seen. The
shepherd came, and saw a dozen
murdered Sheep, but no dog-tracks,
for the scurrying flock had tram-
pled them out. The circumstan-
tial evidence was complete. Many
Sheep had suffered before this time,
and vowing deadly vengeance on all
Foxes, the shepherd set about a plan.

At first he found few to join him,
but more Sheep were killed in
March, including a number of early
lambs, and though some pretended
that they saw large dog-tracks about
the scene of the murder, there were
many who believed the Fox had
done it, and were specially ready
to join in the chase when assured
that the malefactor was none but
the Silver Fox.

XIX

THE PRESERVER OF SNOWYRUFF

HE folk of the upper Shawban were all astir. A great Fox-hunt had been organized. The men who had lost lambs were going because they wanted that Fox killed; the boys were there for sport, and all were there because this was a prime Silver Fox. "I think I know just what to do with the coin if he comes my way," said one. "I 'd

be glad to lift the mortgage off our farm with a day's sport," said another. "That black fox robe means a new team to me," said a third; and so they talked.

The Jukes were not there. They had not lost any lambs, and there was bad feeling between them and the Bentons, who organized the hunt. Abner Jukes was elsewhere engaged,—was on another hunt indeed,—and his Hekla of course was not with the enemy.

A Yankee farmer fox-hunt is a barbarous affair. Every man carries a gun of some kind. The object is to kill the Fox with least damage to the fur. There may be twenty boys and only three or

four Hounds. Such, indeed, was the company that went forth that March morning on the upper Shawban.

Foxes may make a new den every year, but sometimes return to the old one if it has proved a place of quiet and of pleasant memories. Thanks to their eternal vigilance, no foe had found them yet in the aspen-dale. So again the month of March found Snowyruff and Domino clearing out the old den and preparing for the new event.

Because this was their home, they were careful to invite no hostile notice. They came and went with care. They hunted only in far places. Snowyruff was

The Awakening Moon

prowling among the dales of the upper river when the Hounds came on her trail, and giving good tongue, they led away. The farm-boys do not attempt to follow. They scatter to points of view. Their plan is to keep in touch with the Hounds by the baying, then race across country to commanding places, or narrow passes, that the Fox is headed for, and shoot him as he runs by. For the Fox usually goes in a circle around his home region.

The far-reaching hunting-cry of the Hounds was the signal for the boys to scramble to the highest lookout, there to form their opinion of the line of hunt, and each post himself at what he thinks the likeliest place for a shot.

The nearing bay left Snowyruff no doubt of what was doing, and she loped down the sheltered valley of Benton's Creek. Crossing and recrossing by the many log bridges, a plan which would surely delay the Hounds, at first she sped away so fast that the trail had time to cool somewhat. On a dry day it would have been lost, but this, unfortunately, was a day of deep snow, warm winds, and heavy thaw. The creek was a whizzing torrent, the snow was slush, and the Fox went floundering at every bound. The Hounds had a red-hot scent, and their longer legs gave them the advantage.

The speed of her opening run

was slackening, and the start she had added to at first was dwindling now. So far she had eluded the gunners, but it was clear that she could not hold out much longer; the snow got softer as the sun came blazing down, and by degrees her tail sank low. This truly is the Fox's danger, and the measure of his strength. A strong, brave Fox bears his tail aloft in the chase. If his courage fails, the brush droops: in wet snow-time it gets wet and heavy, then droops still more. It drags at last, soaks up wet and slush, and becomes a load that helps to hasten the end. Thus the strong heart lives the longest; the faint heart falls by the way. Snowyruff had never lacked cour-

age, but the snow was very wet and
deep, and, in only a few days more,
a new brood of little Foxes was ex-
pected. What wonder that, as her
strength was spent, her heart should
fail? She was again crossing the
freshet creek by a slender tree when
her foot slipped, and she plunged
into the flood. She swam out
quickly, of course, but now, weighted
with water, her case was indeed a
hard one. There seemed no hope;
it was little more than a despairing
cry she gave as she topped the
next ridge, but it brought an answer,
— the short, sharp bark of the Dog-
fox,— and the Domino, strong and
brave, came like a black hawk
skimming across the snow. She had
no means of telling him her plight,

but she had no need. He sensed it, and did what only the rarest, noblest partners do—took up her burden, followed her trail, and went back to meet the Hounds. This did not mean that he meant to sacrifice himself, but that he felt confidence in his powers that he could cut off the Hounds and lead them far away, while she might go quietly home.

XX

THE STRONG HEART TRIED

BACK for half a mile
he went and the pack
was coming very near
—only three hundred
yards away and run-
ning fast—only two hundred now,
and he lingered, then he began to
trot away from them on the trail
of his mate. But he lingered still,
for what?—to make sure, by a
view! and whether he wished them
to see him, or he merely wished

to see them is not clear, but the effect was the same. At one hundred and fifty yards they viewed each other. The pack burst into the clamor that spreads the news, they quit the trail and flashed after the Fox in sight, and he as quickly disappeared. But at the place they got his scent and here to their credit be it told—they knew that now they were leaving the trail of a tender mother, to take up the trail of a strong Dog-fox; yet there is in their nature an instinctive feeling that this is the right thing to do. The Domino went slowly, for he wished to make certain of them; he showed himself again, and now that the chase was surely his he led them far from the way

his mate had taken. He crossed
the open snow; there were glasses
among the hunters and they were
wildly excited when the news went
forth that they had started the Silver Fox. The boys knew the country; they were posted at every
pass. But there is a something
that cherishes the wild things,—
a something that for lack of a better name we call their *Angel,* and
this silent one with the far-reaching voice was there to keep him.
Only once was he in peril—watching the Dogs too closely he did not
heed the warning of the wind, and
a moment later came a loud report
and a burning sting of shot. One
pellet reached his flank and left a
wound, not deep but galling. He

had seen no hunters, but now the dark Fox knew just what to reckon with.

Now were all his powers alert —now every message read, and the Keeper surely warms to those who hear.

There was every reason that the Domino should go through one or another of the passes, and yet for once in his life his only desire was to keep the hilltops. After three miles, he turned abruptly across the open and followed the railway for twice as far. A mile past the switch he went, and was far ahead; then he walked on the rails back to the switch and took the track that forked. After a long trail there he fearlessly turned toward his home,

tired, sore with the shot-wound, but bearing his tail aloft, as becomes the victor of a hard fight.

He cut across the country of the upper Shawban and, hungry now, was making for a cache in the woods, when he heard sounds that made his heart jump, and, rounding a hill, caught sight of a pack of Hounds, another, a fresh pack, at least thirty in number, with a dozen mounted men; and the wild clamor they made was unmistakable proof that they had found his trail and were after him. There was a time when he might have welcomed such a chase, but, oh, how unfair it was now!

He was wearied and hungry, he was footsore with a chase of hours,

he was galled with a stinging wound, he needed rest. But this, at least, was a real hunt; there were no guns, and a "chase," not a "robe," was what they sought. Yet who can blame the Silver Fox if he made way with his speed indeed, but without the joy of the swift runner that knows that the race is his?

He did not know these hills well; they were far from his usual beat. The hills that he knew were miles away, and among them were the gunners ready at every point, and only too glad to profit by the new relay of hounds. This proved the poorest race he had ever made as a test of cunning, but the hardest he ever entered as a test of strength and speed. It was

round and round the hills for hours, loping steadily on; but the blazing sun had reduced all the snow in the woods to slush. Every ditch was full of ice-cold water; every brook was a freshet. There were pools on all the solid ice, and that great full tail, the strong-heart flag, which on another day might still have been flaunted high, was splashed with wet and mud, and drooped from its very weight. He knew he could wear them down, as he had before, yet he longed for the night, the kindly night. Did he know why? Maybe not to give it clear expression, but the night meant frost, and the frost meant crust, and this would bear the Fox for hours before the Hounds could

run on it. The night indeed meant peace.

Now he was plunging around these hills; his wonderful speed was down to half, but the Hounds were wearing, too. The snow and freshets were too much for the hunters. There were only two remaining, the master of the Hounds, and a tall stripling, Abner Jukes, the only one who knew that the hunted one was the Goldur Silver Fox.

But every advantage was now with the pack; they were closing in. The Domino had no chance to double back. It was straight away; it was wisest to go straight away; so he loped, and loped, and loped, always slower and slower, with

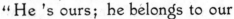

heaving flanks and shortening
bounds and breath, but on and on.
Past one farm-house he went, and
another, then at the doorway of a
third he saw the young Human
Thing with the basket. What is it
that prompts the wild thing in
despair to seek the help of higher
power? Whence comes the deep-
laid impulse in extremity? The
Goldur Fox obeyed the sudden
thought, rushed feebly to the Garden Girl and groveled at her feet.
She seized and dragged him unre-
sisting into the house, then slammed
the door in the face of the pack of
yelling demons. Around the house
they surged and bayed. The hunts-
men came; the farmer came.

"He 's ours; he belongs to our

hounds. They have a right to him; they ran him in here," declared the huntsman.

"He is in my house, and he's mine now," said the farmer, not in the least realizing the quality of the clay-reddened, bedraggled fugitive.

But the farmer had been losing his hens, and he had another weakness; this was easily satisfied, for the robe seemed worn and worthless now, and the hunter was told to "go get his Fox."

"You sha'n't! you sha'n't! He's mine!" cried the girl. "He's my friend. I 've known him for ever so long. You sha'n't kill him!"

The farmer weakened. "We 'll give him fair play," said the huntsman. "We 'll give him a better

start than he had when he came."
And the farmer hurried away that
he might see no more. He could
forget the hunted beast that sought
sanctuary in his house, but he could
not drown that ringing in his ears:
"You sha'n't! you sha'n't! he's
my friend! Oh, Daddy, they are
going to kill him! Oh, Daddy!
Daddy!" And the father's was
not the only heart in which that
childish wail was a scorpion lash
that rankled for long.

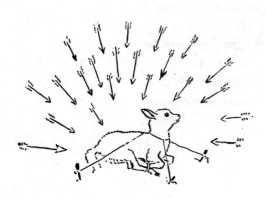

XXI

THE RIVER AND THE NIGHT

BUT they bore him off, and a quarter of a mile of "law" they gave him. "Fair play," they called it — thirty strong Hounds against one worn-out Fox, and the valley rang with baying. Again he bounded over the deep, wet snow, and for a time he won, forging far ahead. Down the long vale of Benton's Creek and across the hillside,

over the ridge and back by the Goldur foot-hills and by a farm-house,
whence out there rushed to join the
pack a long-belated Hound. The
tall hunter welcomed him with a
friendly call. What chance had
Domino now, with this third fresh
relay against him? One chance
alone was left: the night was near;
if only it would come with frost.
But the evening breeze grew milder.
All day the river had been running,
with the warming winds. Now the
Shawban was a mighty, growing
flood of racing, broken ice, filling
the broad valley from brim to brim;
heaving and jarring, it went toward
the west. The sun was setting on
the water-gap away out there. Its
splendor was on a noble scene; this

The
Hunger—
Moon

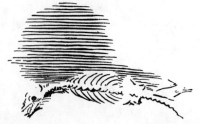

193

surely was the splendid ending of
a noble life.   But neither Hounds
nor hunters stayed to look; it was on
and on.   The Hounds were panting and lunging; their tongues hung
long; their eyes were red.   Far in
the lead was the fresh Hound,— un-
bidden, hateful brute,— and farther
still, the Silver Fox.   That famous
robe was dragged in mud; that
splendid brush was weighted and
sagged with slush; his foot-pads,
worn to the quick, left bloody tracks.
He was wearied as never before.
He might have reached the pathway ledge, but that way was his
home, that way for long a noble instinct said, "Go not."   But now
in direst straits he headed for it, the
one way left.   He rallied his re-

maining power, racing by the
mighty Shawban. His former
speed for a little space was re-
sumed, and he would have won but
that there forged ahead of all the
big, belated Hound, and as he
neared the quarry, bellowed forth
an awful, unmistakable cry—the
horrid, brassy note of Hekla. Who
can measure the speed and start it
took away from the hunted one?
Only this was known: he was
turned, cut off, forced back along
the river-bank, down along the rushing water, now blazing in the low
sun-glow. His hope was gone, but
on he went, his dark form feebly
rocking, knowing he must die, but
fighting for his life. The tall young
huntsman,—the only one in sight,

—now coming on, took in the scene, knew he was at the death, and gazed at the moving blots on the brightness.

O RIVER flashing the red and gold of the red and golden sky, and dappled with blocks of sailing ice! O River of the long chase that ten times before had saved him and dashed red death aside! This is the time of times! Now thirty deaths are on his track, and the track is of feebling bounds. O River of the aspen-dale, will you turn traitor in his dire extremity, thus pen him in, deliver him to his foes?

But the great River went on, mighty, inexorable. Oh, so cruel! And the night came not, but lin-

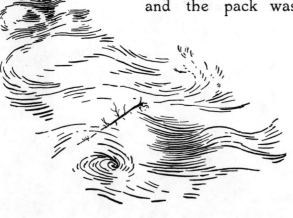

gered. And even as the victim
ran, the fierce, triumphant cry of
all the hunt became a hellish
clamor in his ears. He was worn
out. The brush—the prize and
flag—was no longer borne aloft,
but dragged, wet and heavy, a
menace to his speed; yet still he
loped along the glowing strand.
The Hounds, inspired by victory
in sight, came on bellowing, bounding, blood-mad. To them the
draggled, wounded creature, loping
feebly on the shore, was not a
hunted beast far overmatched, but
a glorious triumph to be reached.

On he went, following, alas! a
point into the stream—a trap, no
less. His River had betrayed him,
and the pack was closing in.

Hekla, howling his deep-voiced hate, was first to block retreat, to corner him at last. It was an open view for all—the broad strand there, with the hunted one; the broad field, with the scattered, yelling pack; the wide River, with its blocks of ice, all rushing on, with death on every side. Here had a faint heart failed and lost; here the strong heart kept on. The surging, roaring pack in Hekla's wake had reached the neck of land, and now came nearer. The surging, roaring River sang as it flowed by the aspen bank. The white Hounds dappled the shore as the white ice dappled the flood; and white they moved together, like mighty teeth to crush the prey.

Closer the ice-blocks came, so that now they mass for a moment, and touch the shore with jar and grating. The hunted turns as though at a sudden thought: better to choose the river death, to die in the River that long had been his friend, and feebly leaping on the ice, from cake to cake, he halted at the last before the plunge. But as he stood, the floe was broken up, was rushed away, with the dark water broadened between; and on that farthest block the dark Fox crouched, riding the white saddle of the black flood. The pack on the shore yelled out their fury, and Hekla, rushing, reached the point of the ice-jam, sprang to the edge, to see the victim sail

away. On the ice he blared his disappointment and his hate, not heeding, not knowing; and the River, irresistible, inexorable, drew swiftly out and whirled away the ice-block whereon he stood. And so they rode together to their doom, the hunted Fox and the hunting Hound. Down they went in that sunset blaze, and on the bank went the pack and the stripling hunter, riding.

A countryman of the other hunt leveled his gun at the Fox; the hunter dashed the gun aside, and cursed the fool. Then there rose on his lips a long halloo, that died, and left the pack in doubt.

At the bend of the River was reached the race, as they call it

—the long reach before the River takes the plunge of Harney's Fall; and there at gaze they stood, the lad and the Hounds, staring into the purple and red sunset and the red and purple River, with blocks of shining ice that bore two living forms away into the blaze. The mists increased with the River's turmoil, the sun-shafts danced more dazzlingly, the golden light turned the ice and the stream and the Silver Fox to gold, as the racing flood and the blazing sky enveloped them from view. The strong heart on the floe gave forth no cry, but the night wind brought the cowering howl of a Hound on whom was the fear of death.

"Good-by, old fellow," said the

THE DEATH RIDE

hunter,—"the stanchest Hound that ever lived!" His voice grew rough. "Good-by, Silver Fox! You have died victorious, as you lived. I wish I could save you both; but what a death you die! Good-by!" Abner saw no more, and the pack on the shore stood shivering and whining.

The shadows fell, the hunter's view was done, but other eyes there were to watch the scene. The current charged fiercely on the last point above the race, and here by reason of the swirl the near blocks took mid-stream, and the middle blocks the farther shore. So the white courser of the hunted one went for a moment grating on the rocks, and Domino saw his chance.

He leaped with all his gathered strength; he cleared the dark and dangerous flood; he landed safe. The River of his youth was the River of his prime.

And away out on the middle floe there came the long-drawn wail of a Hound that knows he is lost. Even as the mists had shut off the view, so now the voice of many waters hushed the cry, and the river keeps its secret to this day.

The Rose Moon

XXII

THE ROSE-MOON

THREE years rolled by on the Shawban. The blessed month of June, the Rose-moon of the woods, was on the land. There are no fairer dales than those of Olabee, over the river. Very beautiful at all times is the dale road, and in this fairest month it seemed the road of Beulah land.

Two lovers were walking hand in

hand, along its pleasant calm. Puritan blood was seen in that tall, square-chinned youth and in the blue-eyed, rosy maid. Goldur memory might have called them up as Hekla's master and the Garden Girl. They came to the sunset ridge, and there sat long to watch the sun go down; and silently they yielded up their hearts to the calm of the day's best hour. It was a time of gentleness and joy, yet was there a shadow between them.

A mother Fox appeared on a flowery bank beside them, and from a hidden home called forth her brood. She fluffed out her snow-white ruff, and as she proudly watched their gambols, another

THE EPILOGUE

form approached, for a moment mere motion in the leaves, and then her mate. He dropped his latest kill and stood erect, a magnificent Silver Fox.

The young man stared intently. He squeezed the hand in his, gave the Girl a quick, significant glance, and whispered: "That's he! He won, he won, but I never knew it till now." Then the only shadow between them faded away.

A last, an unexpected beam of light shone from the water-gap. It blazed and went, a triumph, then a calm. The hidden light glowed so that the dale seemed glad and the Shawban sang, with the aspen-tree, the dear old song of peace.

THE END